W9-ASK-489

MAGIC TREE HOUSE®

MUMMIES IN THE MORNING

MARY POPE OSBORNE'S

MAGIC TREE HOUSE®

MUMMIES IN THE MORNING

ADAPTED BY

JENNY LAIRD

WITH ART BY

KELLY & NICHOLE MATTHEWS

A STEPPING STONE BOOK™

RANDOM HOUSE NEW YORK

This is a work of fiction. Names, characters, places, and incidents either are the product of the author's imagination or are used fictitiously. Any resemblance to actual persons, living or dead, events, or locales is entirely coincidental.

Text copyright © 2022 by Mary Pope Osborne
Art copyright © 2022 by Kelly Matthews & Nichole Matthews
Text adapted by Jenny Laird

All rights reserved. Published in the United States by Random House Children's Books, a division of Penguin Random House LLC, New York. Adapted from *Mummies in the Morning*, published by Random House Children's Books, a division of Penguin Random House LLC, New York, in 1993.

Random House and the colophon are registered trademarks and A Stepping Stone Book and the colophon are trademarks of Penguin Random House LLC. RH Graphic with the book design is a trademark of Penguin Random House LLC. Magic Tree House is a registered trademark of Mary Pope Osborne; used under license.

Visit us on the Web!
rhcbooks.com
MagicTreeHouse.com

Educators and librarians, for a variety of teaching tools, visit us at RHTeachersLibrarians.com

Library of Congress Cataloging-in-Publication Data is available upon request.
ISBN 978-0-593-17479-1 (pb) — ISBN 978-0-593-17476-0 (hc) —
ISBN 978-0-593-17477-7 (lib. bdg.) — ISBN 978-0-593-17478-4 (ebook)

The artists used Clip Studio Paint to create the illustrations for this book.
The text of this book is set in 13-point Cartoonist Hand Regular.

MANUFACTURED IN CHINA
10 9 8 7 6 5 4 3 2 1
First Graphic Novel Edition

This book has been officially leveled by using the F&P Text Level Gradient™ Leveling System.

Random House Children's Books supports the First Amendment and celebrates the right to read. Penguin Random House LLC supports copyright. Copyright fuels creativity, encourages diverse voices, promotes free speech, and creates a vibrant culture. Thank you for buying an authorized edition of this book and for complying with copyright laws by not reproducing, scanning, or distributing any part in any form without permission. You are supporting writers and allowing Penguin Random House to publish books for every reader.

To Georgia and Ada McCulloch
—M.P.O.

For Krish and Alya — a truly magical
brother-and-sister team
—J.L.

To April, our amazing art director, who
has been with us through thick and thin (and
deadlines). Thank you for everything you've
done to offer assistance and advice; this series
wouldn't be the same without you.
—K.M. & N.M.

CHAPTER ONE

Meow!

On a day like any other, in the woods not far from home, Jack and Annie found a mysterious tree house.

FROG CREEK
Hello? Anybody there?

Hello?
It looks empty, Jack.
But I heard a noise. It sounded like someone coughing.
I think it might be coming from over there.
Come on. Let's go up.

M? Are you there?
Why would the mysterious M person be hiding in the bushes?
You can bring them back tomorrow. *Come on!*
Wait for me!
Maybe I should have brought back the medallion.
And the blue bookmark.

I'll bring everything back tomorrow!
SWISH
Everything looks exactly the same as it did yesterday!
Don't touch anything until I get up there.

See? Exactly the same.
BEARS
INDIA
ICE AGE
Samurai
PRIMATES
CRYPT
IV

Hmmm.
Which book is it going to be today?
Hey, this isn't wet anymore.
Let me see.
How is this possible?
It got soaked in the castle moat yesterday.
Maybe the knight who rescued us from the moat also fixed the book.
But... how?

Watch out!
DINOSAURS
Put that away.
Wow! Look at this.
Cool. Pyramids.
PYRAMIDS
And this one has a bookmark, too.

What's that long gold box?
Is that a parade? It looks like a parade.
I don't know. We have to read—

And look! Is that a special kind of cat?
Let's go there! Now!
Let's study the book to find—

I thought you loved pyramids.
I do.
PYRAMIDS
We went to see dinosaurs . . . and you love pyramids more than you love dinosaurs.
Because pyramids can't eat you in one bite.
DINOSAURS
Right! There's nothing scary about pyramids! So let's go see one in real life!
Okay. But find the Pennsylvania book.
In case we want to come straight back here.

Got it!
PENNSYLVANIA STATE
I wish we could go to this place.
Here we go!
WHOOOSH

The tree house started to spin.
It spun faster and faster.

Until everything was still.
Absolutely still.
MEOW!

CHAPTER TWO

Oh, Man. Mummies!

Hi!
Shhh. Someone might hear you.
In the middle of the desert?
Come back!

Oh, wow! Look, Jack!
It's the picture from the book!

What are those people doing?
FLIP
It's an Egyptian funeral.
In a royal funeral, family, servants, and mourners followed the coffin.
The coffin was called a sarcophagus.
That gold box is like a coffin.
It's called a sar . . . sar . . . sar . . .
Oh, forget it.
I'd better make some notes.

Coffin called a S-A-R-C-O-P-H-A-
G-U-S!
Come on, we'd better hurry if we want to see the mummy.
HATS

What mummy?
SARCAPHAGUS
There's probably a mummy in that gold box.
We're in ancient Egypt. Remember?
Oh, man. *Mummies!*
Bye, Jack!

Wait!

HUFF
PUFF
I think my glasses are getting sweaty.

What happened? Where are the people? The gold box? The cat?
They're gone. But the pyramid is still here.
Where did they go?
Maybe they were ghosts.
Annie, there's no such thing as ghosts.

It must have been a mirage.
A what?
Mirage.
It happens in the desert all the time. It looks like something's there.
But it just turns out to be the sunlight bending through hot air.
How could sunlight look like people, a mummy box, and a bunch of cows?
Ghosts.
No way.

Look!
The cat is no mirage.

Where's he going?
Let's find out!

CHAPTER THREE

The Pyramid

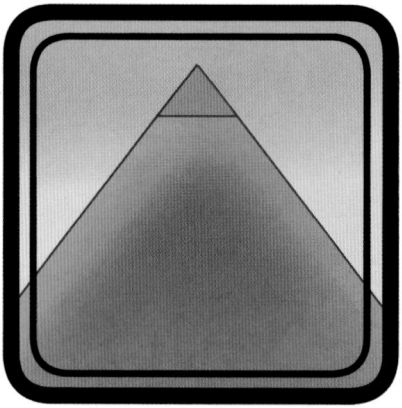

Where did he go?
Let's go in.
Wait!

Let's see what the book says first.
Pyramids were sometimes called Houses of the Dead.
They were almost entirely solid stone, except for the burial chambers deep inside.
Wow. Let's go to the burial chambers. I bet a mummy's in there.
Okay, but stay close behind me.

We have to go farther inside.
I can't see—
Go! Just go!

Here, kitty, kitty!
Shhh. No talking.
I wasn't talking to you, I was talking to the cat.
No talking to the cat . . . or even to yourself.
Come on.

?
I want to look at the book.

The burial chamber is in the middle of the pyramid.

See?
It seems to be straight ahead.

HUFF
PUFF
The floor is flat here. And the air feels different.
Stuffy and old.

I think we're almost to the burial chamber.
Okay, I get it. We were walking uphill, now we're not.
See, the hallway slants up. Then it gets flat.
Then you come to the chamber.
Come on, let's go!

EEEEEEE
CLATTER

CHAPTER FOUR

Back from the Dead

Get down!

CLATTER
A mummy!
Back from the dead!

F-forget it.
Mummies aren't alive.
What's this?

The mummy dropped this thing.
It looks like a scepter.
What's that?
It's a thing kings and queens carry. It means they have power over the people.
Come back, mummy!
We found your scepter.
We want to help you!
Annie! Shhh!

But the mummy—
That was no mummy.
It was a person. A real person.
How do you know?
I saw a foot. A very real foot.
So what kind of person would be inside a pyramid?
Well... we're in here.
Right. Okay, let's see if the book can help us.

"Tomb robbers often stole the treasure buried with mummies.
False passages were sometimes built to stop the robbers."
No live mummy.
Just a tomb robber.
Yikes. A tomb robber?

Yeah, a robber who steals stuff from tombs.
But what if the robber comes back?
We'd better leave.
Right.
But first I want to write something down.

Jack—
Tomb robber
Just a second.
Tomb robber tried to steal
Jack—
Hold on—
Jack, look!

Here, Jack. Give her this.

I—I think this belongs to you.
GASP!
A ghost. A real ghost!

CHAPTER FIVE

The Ghost-Queen

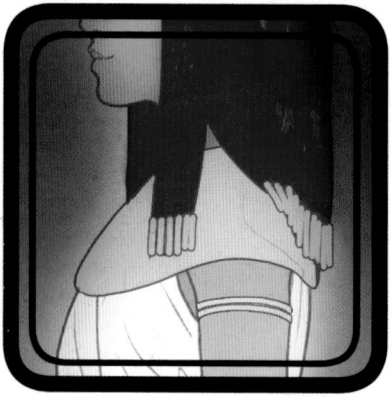

I am Hutepi. Queen of the Nile.
Hi, Hu-Hutepi.
I'm Annie . . . of Frog Creek.
And this is my brother, Jack.
Is it true that you have come to help me?

NUDGE
Right. Help. We're here to help — wait. *We are?*
Yes. Definitely. How can we help?

For a thousand years, I have waited for help.
A thousand years. Wow. That's a long time.
Someone must find my Book of the Dead. I need it to go on to the Next Life.
Why do you need the Book of the Dead?
It will tell me the magic spells I need to get through the Underworld.
The Un-Underworld?

Yes. Before I journey on to the Next Life, I must pass through the horrors of the Underworld.
Poisonous snakes. Lakes of fire. Monsters. Demons.
What kinds of horrors?
Oh.
Yes. I cannot overcome these dangers without the spells in the book.
And the book you're looking for will help keep you safe?
But my brother hid the book so tomb robbers would not steal it.

We saw a tomb robber earlier.
He was trying to steal your scepter but dropped it when he saw us.
If I do not find the book soon, I will never get to the Next Life.
Don't worry, we will help you find the book before the robber gets it.
Right, Jack?
Um. Right. But *how?*

My brother carved this secret message on the wall, telling me how to find it.
Where? Here?
Yes. He carved his message on the only stone in this wall shaped like the eye of a cat.
Cool.
What do these tiny pictures mean?
Alas, my brother forgot my strange problem. I cannot see clearly that which is close to my eyes.
I have not been able to read his message for a thousand years.

Oh, that's not a strange problem. Jack can't see anything, either.
But only when you wear your glasses.
I can, too! I can see everything you can see.
Jack, lend her your glasses.
I fear I cannot wear your glasses, Jack. I am made of air.
Oh, right. I forgot.

But perhaps you will describe the hieroglyphs on this wall.
Hi-ro-who?
Hieroglyphs, Annie.
It's the ancient Egyptian way of writing. It's like writing with pictures.
Thank you, Jack.

Oh, man. These are cool.
There are four pictures here.
Describe them to me, Jack.
One at a time, please.

CHAPTER SIX

The Writing on the Wall

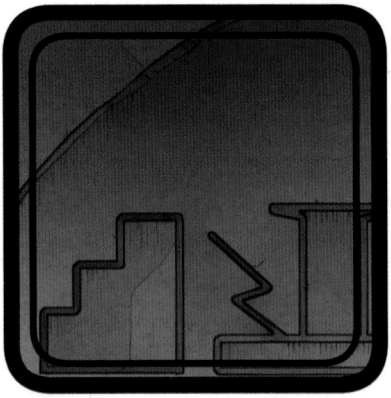

Okay.
The first one is like this.
Like stairs?
Yes, stairs! Just like stairs.
And the second picture?
Oh, right.

Hmm. The second one has a long box on the bottom.
With shapes on top of the box.
? ? ?

There are three shapes.
The first one looks like this.
The second one looks like this . . . like a chimney.
Right. Then the third shape leans on the chimney. Like this . . .
I'm sorry. I do not understand.

Hat?
It looks kind of like a hat.
It's more like a boat.
Boat?
HMMM

Yes, Annie's right. It could be a boat.
A boat. Of course.
Two down. Two more to go.
THUD
Tomb robber?
Perhaps.
We have to hurry.

The third picture is like a thing that holds flowers.
Or a thing that holds water.
Like a jug?
Exactly!

This one is easy. It's a candy cane.
They didn't have candy canes in ancient Egypt.
Oh. Right.
Or like a curved stick. But one side is shorter than the other.
The last one looks like a pole that droops.
Wait!
I have an idea.
I'll draw it in my notebook. Big! So you can see it.
Good idea!

A folded cloth.
Well, not really.
But that is the hieroglyph for a folded cloth.
Hmmph.
I don't see how that's a folded cloth, but okay.

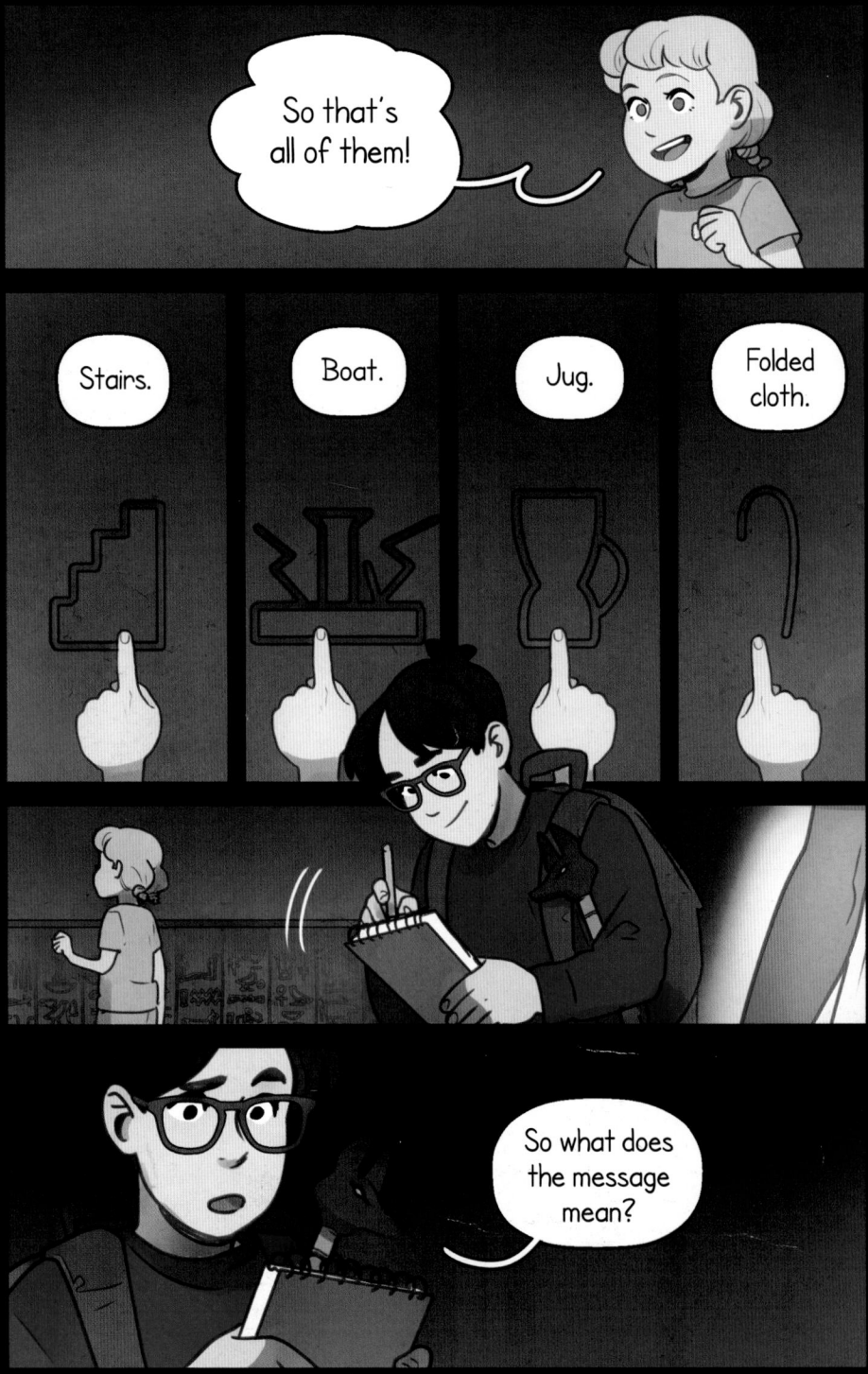
So that's all of them!
Stairs.
Boat.
Jug.
Folded cloth.
So what does the message mean?

Come.
Come to my burial chambers.

CHAPTER SEVEN

The Scroll

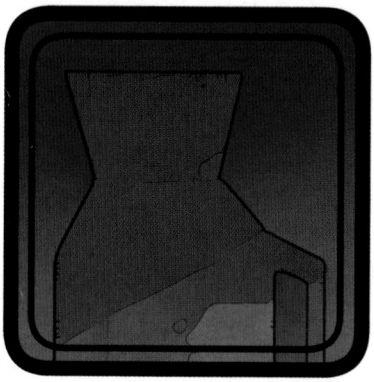

Hurry, before we lose her!

The STAIRS!

CREEAK

Where did she go?
Maybe this is the burial chamber?

Queen Hutepi? Are you here?
Hey, there's the BOAT!
What's it doing inside Queen Hutepi's pyramid?
Maybe it's supposed to carry her to the Next Life.

Look!

The JUG!
Something's in here.
What is it?
It feels like a big napkin.
The FOLDED CLOTH!

But that's the last clue.
Where's the book?

Books from ancient Egypt don't look like our books.
Oh.
What do they look like?
Like this.
ROLL
ROLL

Oh, man.
This must be the Book of the Dead.
We found it!
We found the book!
Now we have to find Queen Hutepi.

Queen Hutepi! We have it!
We found your Book of the Dead!
Shhhh. The tomb robber might hear you.
Oh, right. Sorry.
Queen Hutepi?

Maybe she's in there.
Wait—
Come on, Jack.
No.
She's waited a thousand years for her book.
Don't make her wait anymore.

Just in case it's the tomb robber, I'll hide the book in here.

Hurry, Jack!
Queen Hutepi?
We found it. Your Book of the Dead.

Let's leave the scroll on the floor.
And go.
No. I think we should leave it in there.
No. Way.

Don't be afraid.
You've already seen a ghost, and she turned out to be nice.
That's true.
Come on.
...
Oh, wow!
A real mummy!

CHAPTER EIGHT

The Mummy

Oh, gross!
It's interesting.
I think it's Queen Hutepi.
I'll see what the book says...
Forget it!
Let's go!

You're the one who wanted to see a real mummy!
Now that I've seen one, I want to leave!
Come on, Jack. Hurry!
"Ancient Egyptians tried to protect the body so it would last forever. First it was dried out with salt."
Ugh, stop!
"Next it was covered with oil. Then it was wrapped tightly in bandages. The brain was removed by—"
Yuck!
SHUDDER

Listen. This is interesting—
I'm leaving! Good-bye!
Wait, Annie!
We have to give her the Book of the Dead!
...

Here's your scepter.
I hope this helps you find your way to the Next Life.

SSIIIIIIIIIGHHH
Whoa.

Phew!

Hey! Annie!
Where are you?
Annie?
Annie!

Jack! Help!
You sound far away!
Where are you?
I'm in the hallway!
I'm in the hallway, too! Don't move!
I'm not moving!
Okay! I'll find you!
Annie!
Jack!
Wait!
Now you sound farther away!
I promise, I haven't moved!

!
Annie?!
Jack!
Getting closer!
Where are you?!
I'm close!
Just stay where you are!

Annie!
Jack!
Getting closer!
Annie!
Jack!
Annie! Is that you?!

Jack!
I was lost!
It's okay. You're okay.
What happened?
I think this is one of those false passages.
A false passage?
Yeah. Built to fool the tomb robbers.
See, it looks just like the right hallway.
When you left the room with the boat, you must have gone through the wrong door.
How do we find the right door?

We have to go back into the boat room.
I know where to go from there.
You're so smart.
CREEEEAAK
What was that?

RUMBLE
What's that sound?
I don't know.
RUMB
WHOOOOSSH!!

CHAPTER NINE

Follow the Leader

What happened?
I don't know. Something weird.
We have to get out of here. Fast.
The stairs are right here.
KICK KICK
Take my hand.
We'll climb up and see if we can push open the door.
Good idea.

Keep your other hand on the wall.
Got it.
Don't worry. Everything's going to be okay.
Of course.
Here it is! I feel the door.
Let's push as hard as we can.
PUUUUSSSHH
It won't budge.

Let's try again.
NOD
PUUUSSHH!!
It's . . . no . . . use.
What can we do?
Let's just rest a moment.
SLUMP
Let's look for another exit.
But we can't see anything.

Come on. Just like before.
Here's the floor.
Which way do we go?
This way, I think.

I'll feel the wall for corners. You stay just behind me.
Hold on to my hand.
No letting go.

Hold on. A corner. Turn right here.
Ah! Here's another corner.
This way.
This is like a maze.
I'm glad you're good at mazes.

Hold on.
I think this might be more stairs.
Let's see if there's a door at the top.
Yep. Stairs.
KICK
KICK

Here's a door. Feel it?
Let's push.
Yes.
PUSH!
Let's try it with our backs.
PUSH!
This one won't budge, either.
Jack... what if this is the same door we started at?
What if we're trapped?

SQUEEZE
Oh, man.
Meow.
He's back!
Hurry! Follow him!
He knows the way!

Where did he go?
Meow.
This way!
Meow.
Turn left here.
Meow.

Meow.
Meow.
Careful, it's steep here.
We must be getting close.

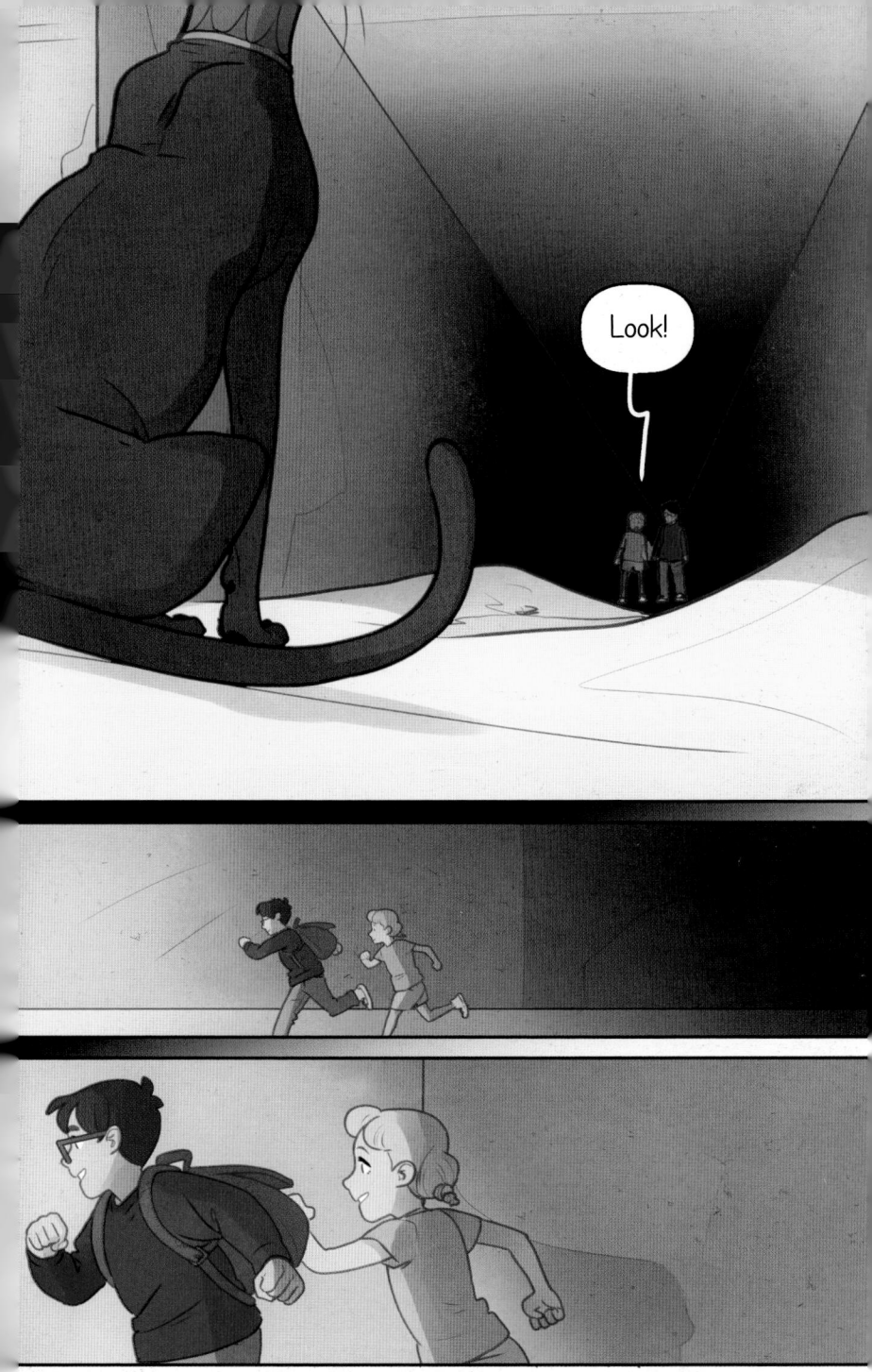
Look!

YAY!
YAY!

Which way is the tree house?
Annie . . .
How did we get out of the false passage?

The cat.
But how could the cat do it?
Magic.

But—
Look! Over there!

Thank you!
Thanks!

Time to go home.
HUFF
PUFF

Jack?
Yeah?
It's okay. You didn't know it was a false passage.
I'm sorry I ran away.
I was just going to wait for you at the bottom of the stairs.
But you figured it out. If you didn't love to read, you might not have found me.
I might have been lost in there for a thousand years.
Then I would have searched the pyramid for a thousand years.
I would never leave you behind, Annie. You're my sister!

Did you give Queen Hutepi her book?
Yes. And the scepter.
Did anything happen?
Not really. But . . .
But, what?
When I gave her the book, the mummy seemed almost . . . happy.
I hope that means Queen Hutepi is finally able to make her journey.
Me too.

Where did we put the Pennsylvania book?
MYT
Islands

Here it is.
RUMBLE
RUMBLE
Hey, that's the same sound we heard in the pyramid.
ROBOTS

Wow! That's the coolest mirage ever!
Maybe it's not a mirage.
Right. Maybe Queen Hutepi is finally on her way to the Next Life.

Good-bye, Queen Hutepi.
We hope the book helps you.
It will. I know it will.
We wish we could go home!
WH
SH
OOO

The tree house started to spin.
It spun faster and faster.
Until everything was still.
Absolutely still.

CHAPTER TEN

Another Clue

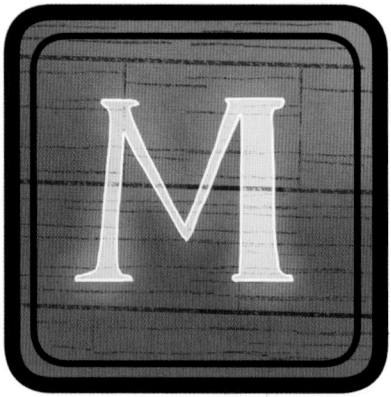

I wonder what Mom's making for lunch.
I hope it's peanut butter and jelly sandwiches.
Boy, this place is a mess. We'd better make it neater. In case M comes back.
I hope we get to meet the mysterious M person. I have so many questions I want to ask.
Let's make a pile of all our adventures so far.
Good idea.

I'll put the Egypt book on the bottom.
Then the dinosaur book.
Yeah, good.
The castle book can go on top.
Knights and Castles
I know it's weird, but I feel like the knight is our friend.
It's not weird. He helped us.
That's what friends do.

!
Yeah, and the Pteranodon helped us in dinosaur times.
And the cat in Egypt!
Annie, you were right!
I was?
Yes, maybe the cat was magic! And the Pteranodon and the knight.
Maybe the M person sent them to help us.

Jack. Look!
What is it?
You have to see for yourself.
I don't see anything.
Turn your head a little.
You have to catch the light just right.

The letter M!
This proves the tree house belongs to M!
Is it a mirage or is it real?
It's real. And a mirage.
At the same time.

WHOOOOOOSSH
Let's go down now.

RUSTLE
RUSTLE
Who's there?
I'm going to bring the medallion back soon!
And the bookmark, too.
Both of them. Tomorrow!
Do you think M is in the bushes?
Or somewhere close by.
Should we look for M?

Ja-ack! An-nie!
We'll look for M tomorrow!

STOP

You're just in time for lunch.

Missed the first adventure? Get whisked back to the time of dinosaurs with Jack and Annie in . . .

Dinosaurs Before Dark Graphic Novel excerpt text copyright © 2021 by Mary Pope Osborne. Adapted by Jenny Laird. Cover art and interior illustrations copyright © 2021 by Kelly & Nichole Matthews. Published by Random House Children's Books, a division of Penguin Random House LLC, New York.

Where Is Here?

Are you okay?
I'm okay. Are you?
Magicia
Mars
Jungles
Yeah.
Okay. Yeah.
That was weird.

What happened?
I don't know.
Do those leaves look different?
Not to me.

Um, Annie?
DINOSAURS

Where are we?
DINOSAURS
It's the same.
Yeah, *exactly* the same.
Except real...
and alive.
DINOSAURS

Even that bird matches!
That's not a bird.
It's a flying reptile. A Pteranodon.
A what-a-don?

Just call it a dinosaur.
Cool!
A dinosaur!
No, wait... none of this can be real.
DINOSAURS

DINOSAURS
But he's real, Jack.
He's very real.

Hi!
Shhhh.
We're not supposed to be here.
But where is here?
I–I don't know.

Where is here?
He can't understand you, Annie.
And he definitely can't talk.
But maybe the book can tell us.
This flying reptile lived in the Cretaceous Period. It vanished 65 million years ago.
DINOSAURS
65 million years ago?
This is impossible!

Jack, he's nice.
Nice?
Yeah, I can tell.
Let's go down and talk to him.
Talk to him?
Hey!
Dragons
Ninjas

Annie, no!
Wait!

Gasp!

LET THE MAGIC TREE HOUSE® WHISK YOU AWAY!

Read all the novels in the #1 bestselling chapter book series of all time!

TRACK THE FACTS WITH JACK & ANNIE!
MAGIC TREE HOUSE FACT TRACKER
Dinosaurs
Will Osborne and Mary Pope Osborne
MAGIC TREE HOUSE FACT TRACKER
Knights and Castles
Will Osborne and Mary Pope Osborne
MAGIC TREE HOUSE FACT TRACKER
Mummies and Pyramids
Will Osborne and Mary Pope Osborne
MAGIC TREE HOUSE FACT TRACKER
Pirates
Will Osborne and Mary Pope Osborne
MAGIC TREE HOUSE FACT TRACKER
Rain Forests
Will Osborne and Mary Pope Osborne
MAGIC TREE HOUSE FACT TRACKER
Space
Will Osborne and Mary Pope Osborne
MAGIC TREE HOUSE FACT TRACKER
Titanic
Will Osborne and Mary Pope Osborne
MAGIC TREE HOUSE FACT TRACKER
Twisters and Other Terrible Storms
Will Osborne and Mary Pope Osborne
MAGIC TREE HOUSE FACT TRACKER
Dolphins and Sharks
Mary Pope Osborne and Natalie Pope Boyce
MAGIC TREE HOUSE FACT TRACKER
Ancient Greece and the Olympics
Mary Pope Osborne and Natalie Pope Boyce
MAGIC TREE HOUSE FACT TRACKER
American Revolution
Mary Pope Osborne and Natalie Pope Boyce
MAGIC TREE HOUSE FACT TRACKER
Sabertooths and the Ice Age
Mary Pope Osborne and Natalie Pope Boyce
MAGIC TREE HOUSE FACT TRACKER
Pilgrims
Mary Pope Osborne and Natalie Pope Boyce
MAGIC TREE HOUSE FACT TRACKER
Ancient Rome and Pompeii
Mary Pope Osborne and Natalie Pope Boyce
MAGIC TREE HOUSE FACT TRACKER
Tsunamis and Other Natural Disasters
Mary Pope Osborne and Natalie Pope Boyce
MAGIC TREE HOUSE FACT TRACKER
Polar Bears and the Arctic
Mary Pope Osborne and Natalie Pope Boyce
MAGIC TREE HOUSE FACT TRACKER
Sea Monsters
Mary Pope Osborne and Natalie Pope Boyce

MAGIC TREE HOUSE
FACT TRACKER
Penguins and Antarctica
Mary Pope Osborne and Natalie Pope Boyce

MAGIC TREE HOUSE
FACT TRACKER
Leonardo da Vinci
Monday with a Mad Genius!
Mary Pope Osborne and Natalie Pope Boyce

MAGIC TREE HOUSE
FACT TRACKER
Ghosts
A Good Night for Ghosts
Mary Pope Osborne and Natalie Pope Boyce

MAGIC TREE HOUSE
FACT TRACKER
Leprechauns and Irish Folklore
Mary Pope Osborne and Natalie Pope Boyce

MAGIC TREE HOUSE
FACT TRACKER
Rags and Riches
Kids in the Time of Charles Dickens
Mary Pope Osborne and Natalie Pope Boyce

MAGIC TREE HOUSE
FACT TRACKER
Snakes and Other Reptiles
A Crazy Day with Cobras
Mary Pope Osborne and Natalie Pope Boyce

MAGIC TREE HOUSE
FACT TRACKER
Dog Heroes
Dogs in the Dead of Night
Mary Pope Osborne and Natalie Pope Boyce

MAGIC TREE HOUSE
FACT TRACKER
Abraham Lincoln
Abe Lincoln at Last!
Mary Pope Osborne and Natalie Pope Boyce

MAGIC TREE HOUSE
FACT TRACKER
Pandas and Other Endangered Species
A Perfect Time for Pandas
Mary Pope Osborne and Natalie Pope Boyce

MAGIC TREE HOUSE
FACT TRACKER
Horse Heroes
Stallion by Starlight
Mary Pope Osborne and Natalie Pope Boyce

MAGIC TREE HOUSE
FACT TRACKER
Heroes for All Times
High Time for Heroes
Mary Pope Osborne and Natalie Pope Boyce

MAGIC TREE HOUSE
FACT TRACKER
Soccer
Soccer on Sunday
Mary Pope Osborne and Natalie Pope Boyce

MAGIC TREE HOUSE
FACT TRACKER
Ninjas and Samurai
Night of the Ninjas
Mary Pope Osborne and Natalie Pope Boyce

MAGIC TREE HOUSE
FACT TRACKER
China
Land of the Emperor's Great Wall
Day of the Dragon King
Mary Pope Osborne and Natalie Pope Boyce

MAGIC TREE HOUSE
FACT TRACKER
Sharks and Other Predators
Sunset of the Shark
Mary Pope Osborne and Natalie Pope Boyce

MAGIC TREE HOUSE
FACT TRACKER
Vikings
Mary Pope Osborne and Natalie Pope Boyce

MAGIC TREE HOUSE
FACT TRACKER
Dogsledding and Extreme Sports
Mary Pope Osborne and Natalie Pope Boyce

MAGIC TREE HOUSE
FACT TRACKER
Dragons and Mythical Creatures
Night of the Ninth Dragon
Mary Pope Osborne and Natalie Pope Boyce

MAGIC TREE HOUSE
FACT TRACKER
World War II
Mary Pope Osborne and Natalie Pope Boyce

MAGIC TREE HOUSE
FACT TRACKER
Baseball
Mary Pope Osborne and Natalie Pope Boyce

MAGIC TREE HOUSE
FACT TRACKER
Wild West
Mary Pope Osborne and Natalie Pope Boyce

MAGIC TREE HOUSE
FACT TRACKER
Texas
Mary Pope Osborne and Natalie Pope Boyce

MAGIC TREE HOUSE
FACT TRACKER
Warriors
Warriors in Winter
Mary Pope Osborne and Natalie Pope Boyce

MAGIC TREE HOUSE
FACT TRACKER
Benjamin Franklin
To the Future, Ben Franklin!
Mary Pope Osborne and Natalie Pope Boyce

MAGIC TREE HOUSE
FACT TRACKER
Narwhals and Other Whales
Mary Pope Osborne and Natalie Pope Boyce

MARY POPE OSBORNE is the author of many novels, picture books, story collections, and nonfiction books. Her #1 *New York Times* bestselling Magic Tree House® series has been translated into numerous languages around the world. Highly recommended by parents and educators everywhere, the series introduces young readers to different cultures and times, as well as to the world's legacy of ancient myth and storytelling.

JENNY LAIRD is an award-winning playwright. She collaborates with Will Osborne and Randy Courts on creating musical theater adaptations of the Magic Tree House® series for both national and international audiences. Their work also includes shows for young performers, available through Music Theatre International's Broadway Junior® Collection. Currently the team is working on a Magic Tree House® animated television series.

KELLY & NICHOLE MATTHEWS are twin sisters and a comic-art team. They get to do their dream job every day, drawing comics for a living. They've worked with Boom Studios!, Archaia, the Jim Henson Company, Hiveworks, and now Random House!